Ladybird books are widely available, but in case of
difficulty may be ordered by post or telephone from:

Ladybird Books – Cash Sales Department
Littlegate Road Paignton Devon TQ3 3BE
Telephone 0803 554761

A catalogue record for this book is available
from the British Library

Published by Ladybird Books Ltd Loughborough Leicestershire UK

THE TALE OF
MRS
TIGGY-WINKLE™

Based on the original and authorized story
by Beatrix Potter
Ladybird Books in association with Frederick Warne

Once upon a time, there was a little girl called Lucie, who lived at a farm called Little-town. She was a good little girl only she was *always* losing her pocket handkerchiefs!

One day Lucie came running into the farmyard crying, "I've lost my pocket-handkin. That's three handkins and a pinafore. Oh, dear! Have *you* seen them, Tabby Kitten?"

The kitten went on washing her paws,
so Lucie asked a speckled hen. "Sally
Henny-penny, have *you* found three
pocket-handkins?"

But the hen ran into a barn. "I go
barefoot, barefoot, barefoot," she
clucked.

"Well, that wasn't very helpful,"
sighed Lucie.

So she asked Cock Robin. But he just looked sideways at Lucie, and then flew over a stile towards the hill behind Little-town.

Lucie climbed onto the stile. Way up on the hill she thought she saw some white things spread upon the grass. "They might just be my lost handkins!" she cried.

Lucie scrambled up a steep pathway as fast as her stout little legs would carry her.

Soon she came to a spring bubbling out of the hillside. Where the sand on the path was wet, there were footmarks – very *small* footmarks!

Lucie followed the little footmarks until she came to a big rock. Here the grass was short and green, and there was a heap of tiny clothes pegs – but no pocket handkerchiefs.

Suddenly Lucie noticed a tiny door. Behind the door, she could hear someone singing.

Lucie knocked once – twice, and interrupted the song. A small, frightened voice called out, "Who's that?"

Lucie opened the door and walked into a tiny kitchen. Everything inside the kitchen was so very small – even the pots and pans!

And there, picking up an iron near the fire, was a very stout, short person. Her little black nose went sniffle, sniffle, snuffle, and her eyes went twinkle, twinkle. And beneath her cap, that little person had – *prickles*!

"Forgive me, I didn't mean to startle you, but who are *you*?" asked Lucie. "And have you seen my pocket-handkins?"

"Oh, yes, if you please'm. My name is Mrs Tiggy-winkle." She took something out of her clothes basket, and spread it over an ironing blanket.

"What's that?" asked Lucie. "That's not my pocket-handkin."

"Oh no, if you please'm. That's a little scarlet waistcoat belonging to Cock Robin." Mrs Tiggy-winkle ironed the waistcoat, folded it and put it to one side.

Then Mrs Tiggy-winkle took something from her clothes horse.

"That isn't my pinny," said Lucie.

"Oh no, if you please'm. That's a tablecloth belonging to Jenny Wren," replied Mrs Tiggy-winkle. "Look how it's stained with currant wine. It's very bad to wash." Then Mrs Tiggy-winkle fetched another hot iron from the fire.

Lucie knelt down and began to look through Mrs Tiggy-winkle's clothes basket. "There's one of my pocket-handkins!" she cried. "And look, there's my pinny."

"Fancy that, they were there all the time. I knew I'd got them somewhere," said Mrs Tiggy-winkle, as she ironed the pinny and shook out the frills.

"Oh, that *is* lovely," said Lucie.

"Goodness, what are *they*?" she asked, pointing to some long yellow things Mrs Tiggy-winkle was holding. "They seem to have fingers instead of feet, or are they gloves?"

"Oh, that's a pair of stockings belonging to Sally Henny-penny. Look how she's worn the heels out with scratching in the yard," said Mrs Tiggy-winkle. "She'll very soon go barefoot!

"And this handkin belongs to old Mrs Rabbit," she continued. "It *did* so smell of onions! I've had to wash it separately."

"There's another one of my handkins!" cried Lucie suddenly.

Mrs Tiggy-winkle ironed the handkerchief and folded it and put it to one side.

"And what are those funny little things?" asked Lucie.

"A pair of mittens belonging to Tabby Kitten. I only have to iron them, she washes them herself," replied Mrs Tiggy-winkle, and she bent down to pick up something else from her clothes basket. It was Lucie's last handkerchief.

"And what are you doing now?" asked Lucie.

"I always have to starch these little dicky shirt-fronts. They're Tom Titmouse's and he's most terrible particular," said Mrs Tiggy-winkle. "There now, I've finished my ironing and I'll just hang these up to air."

Mrs Tiggy-winkle climbed onto a chair and hung up all sorts and sizes of clothes on her clothesline – small brown coats of mice, one velvety black moleskin waistcoat, a red tail-coat with no tail belonging to Squirrel Nutkin, and a very much shrunk, blue jacket belonging to Peter Rabbit. At last the basket was empty and Mrs Tiggy-winkle's work done.

Then Mrs Tiggy-winkle and Lucie sat down to take some tea. Mrs Tiggy-winkle poured tea into two cups – a cup for herself and a cup for Lucie.

They sat before the warm, friendly fire and looked sideways at one another.

All through Mrs Tiggy-winkle's gown and cap, there were *hairpins* sticking wrong end out, so that Lucie didn't like to sit too near her!

When they had finished their tea, they tied up all the clothes in bundles. Lucie's pocket handkerchiefs were folded up inside her clean pinny and fastened with a silver safety pin.

Mrs Tiggy-winkle made up the fire with turf. Then she and Lucie came out, locked the door and hid the key under the door-sill.

"Now to deliver the washing," said Mrs Tiggy-winkle.

Down the hill trotted Lucie and Mrs Tiggy-winkle with the bundles of clean clothes.

All the way down the path little animals and birds came out of the fern to meet them. The very first little animals they met were Peter Rabbit and Benjamin Bunny.

Mrs Tiggy-winkle gave them their fresh, clean clothes.

Then all the other little animals and birds came closer to say 'thank you' to dear Mrs Tiggy-winkle for their clean clothes.

Soon Mrs Tiggy-winkle and Lucie reached the bottom of the hill, and by the time they had come to the stile, there was nothing left to carry except Lucie's one little bundle.

Lucie scrambled up the stile with
the bundle in her hand. She turned
to say good night, and to thank the
washerwoman – but what a very odd
thing! Mrs Tiggy-winkle had not
waited either for thanks or to give
Lucie the bill for washing her clothes.

Lucie watched Mrs Tiggy-winkle running, running, running up the hillside. "But where is your cap, your shawl and your gown?" she said to herself.

Lucie could hardly believe her eyes!

Mrs Tiggy-winkle had grown very small – and very brown – and was covered with – *prickles*!

"Why! If I didn't know better, Mrs Tiggy-winkle, I should think that you were nothing but a *hedgehog*!" cried Lucie.

Lucie wondered if she had been dreaming. But if she were, how could she be carrying three clean handkerchiefs, wrapped in her pinny and fastened with a silver safety pin?